Pendulum

University of Pittsburgh at Greensburg

Spring 2024

Pendulum Literary Magazine is a student-run publication
accepting submissions from students at the University of Pittsburgh at Greensburg.
Pendulum wishes to thank Al Thiel, Lori Jakiela, and Dave Newman.

A Letter from the Editor

Over the last three years I have helped to publish three issues of Pendulum. Over that time, Pendulum has published beautiful stories about families and relationships, heartbreaking poems about loss and regret, and black and white photos that do the impossible: capture the beauty of Greensburg.

We have been so lucky to feature a wide variety of students in this edition of Pendulum. Creative writing majors share the page with business majors, and first-year students appear alongside graduating seniors.

The Spring 2024 edition of Pendulum is the longest since my being Editor-in-Chief, featuring 22 contributors and 53 pieces. I am so proud of this collection, as it shows the true heart of the Pitt-Greensburg community.

I hope you are proud too.

Caitlin Cruser
Editor-in-Chief

Table of Contents
Poetry and Prose

Rin Alford
    I See You in the Lunch Line   6
    Empty Cup   8
    Where I'm From   9
Francis Blubaugh
    Thank You God   11
McKenzie Bonar
    The Female Experience   13
    Birthday Wish   14
    A Doll's World   16
Autumn Buchheit
    Wildflower   17
Kate Cramer
    I am From Everything   18
    A Pirate's Note Home   20
Caitlin Cruser
    two friends and I got haircuts on thursday   21
    when I hear the word 'yinz'   23
    annie   24
Cole Drusbasky
    Poetry and Bourbon   25
    The Dad Image   26
Sone Ekukole-Sone
    Daddy's Drugs   27
Orlando Gannon
    On Dying   32
    Following the Wrong God Home   33
    Reflections   35
    Hunting Tigers   37
Sophia Gatti
    mt. washington outlook//pittsburgh, pa   41
    cigarette butts   42
Monroe Harris
    led down the primrose path   43

Table of Contents

Julia Hills
    Learning to Drive with my Mostly Deaf Grandad...   45
    Aging on the Internet   46
Lauren Hohol
    Siblings   47
Jeannette Hutzell
    The Dog Didn't Actually Die That Year, By The Way...   53
    An Old Hag   54
    Small Town U.S.A.   55
Benjamin Keslar
    Death and Taxes   57
Jed Kudrick
    Level Green as Baseball   62
    The Fall: Monroeville: 18   63
    The Glass   65
Alexis Osborne
    Spotlight   68
Alexander Ray
    Death of Moral   69
    Reflection   71
    Autumn   72
Geneva Webber-Smith
    ER waiting room   73
    what are the twenty-something flavors in a Dr. Pepper?   74
    Thank You Doctor Manning   75
Eleanor Withers
    Paper Accordions and Pigs in Spaceships   78
    Late Night Creations in the Bottom Bunk   80
Florence Zhang
    Dear T,   81
    My Father Now Resting   82
    The Good Old Dogs   83

Table of Contents
Art and Photography

Cole Drusbasky
- Somewhere in Greenburg ... 39
- Somewhere Else in Greenburg ... 40
- Brayden ... 56

Lauren Hohol
- Fog Along the Footbridge ... 76
- Forge Ahead ... 77

Ceili Schiller
- Overgrowth ... 84
- Tandem Living ... 85

Rin Alford

I See You in the Lunch Line

But your head turns,
and I realize it can't be,
because you had a beard,
and he doesn't.

I see you again as I walk
to a class we were meant to share,
my breath gets caught in my throat,
but it isn't you.

I see you at the store
when I go to buy chocolate,
and I see you
in a heart-shaped valentine's box.

I see you in a pint of beer.
I see you in my back seat,
in the pink shoebox
filled with trading cards.

I see you in my room,
sitting on the carpet,
eating Taco Bell
and smoking your pen.

I see you now,
in class, one of those seats
is supposed to be yours,
should have been.

Rin Alford

Your name is still on the roster,
even days after your death,
the teacher calls your name,
then scratches a pen, marking you absent.

Rin Alford

Empty Cup

Tea leaves sink
to the bottom
Conversation lulls
and we become silent.

The rays hit your face,
and I take you in.
The greens of your iris
hair faded with colors
from multiple dye jobs.

But all too soon the moment is cut–
I'm taken out of my haze
as you stand and
leave a tip.
A few coins.

I want to take your hand
or maybe your wrist
anything to keep you here.

But you give me a smile,
and I know
this is our end.

So I smile
and stay seated
as you walk out.

I sip on cold tea.

Rin Alford

Where I'm From

I am from brightly colored nights,
from fried foods and loud cheers of fun,
I am from the sound of trucks moving at night,
from state lines that blur as we pass them by.

I am from the small house that was identical to the ones connected to it,
the ones that hosted loud parties of drunken people.
I am from the backyard of the neighbors' kids,
with bushes full of poisonous berries.

I am from the rental down the road from that house.
An upgrade in space but a downgrade in friends.
I am from the boxes that were never unpacked until they were put on a truck again.

I am from the same state but a different town.
I am from sweaty karate lessons, filled with local kids,
the kind who believed in the second coming of Hitler.
I am from the backyard filled with gravel,
With a forest just beyond it.
The same forest that lit up with fireflies on a stormy night.

I am from industrial smoke and broken buildings.
Streets filled with people hoping for spare change.
I am from a neighborhood filled with kids who knew what it meant to fight,
who knew a knife better than they knew their family.

I am from the roads that go on endlessly,
the smell of cardboard and packing tape.
From the sound of things shifting around,
the wind rattling the car as it speeds down the road,
radios that play hits from the 2000's.

Rin Alford

I am from rest stations that sell cheap burgers and expensive coffees,
the smell of gasoline and lines of trucks filling the second lot.

I am from nowhere and everywhere,
a world of endless possibility at the cost of never settling down.

Francis Blubaugh

Thank You God

In the heart of the wilderness, where the air breathes free,
Among the whispering pines and the buzzing of the bee,
Lived a world untouched, pristine in its glow,
A father and daughter, in nature's embrace, in tow.

They stepped out from their haven, into the wild's embrace,
Where sunlight danced through leaves, a tranquil, hallowed space.
The father, tall and kind, with eyes that sparkled bright,
The daughter, a burst of joy, a sparrow in her flight.

Hand in hand they ventured, through the verdant maze,
Giggles echoed in the woods, as in the open glade they'd gaze.
The father's heart swelled with pride, his treasure by his side,
In this moment, nothing else mattered, in nature's endless tide.

The game they played was simple, a chase of laughter and cheer,
As the daughter ran with glee, her father was always near.
But fate, in its silent tread, had laid a trap unseen,
What was a rusty nail, cruel and sharp, amidst the forest green.

With a step, the world shifted, pain searing through,
As the father's foot met metal, piercing the flesh through and through.
Three inches deep it struck, a testament to his pain,
Yet, not a cry he uttered, his composure he did maintain.

The daughter turned, her eyes wide, fear and worry in her gaze,
But the father, with a smile, met her look with an unwavering blaze.
"Thank You God," he whispered, a prayer amidst the sting,
Grateful for this burden, that to him and not her did this fate bring it to
    be.

Francis Blubaugh

Not to his precious child, whose steps were light and free,
But to him, the shield and guardian, as a father's meant to be.
His pain, a small price to pay, for the safety of his kin,
A lesson in this sharp encounter, a reminder from within.

"Be careful, my dear," he spoke, his voice but a tender song,
"This world is full of beauty, but dangers too belong.
Let this be our lesson, in our adventures to come,
To watch, to care, to protect, under the sun."

The daughter, with tears brimming, yet strength in her young heart,
Approached her father, her hero, from whom she'd never part.
In her eyes, the father saw love, trust, and a bond so strong,
In that moment of shared pain, they knew they belong.

As they returned back to their home, through the trees standing tall,
The wilderness around them had been a witness to it all.
In that rusty nail's piercing, a story was born,
Of love, sacrifice, and care, a bond forever sworn.

"Thank You God," father said, as he closed his eyes in peace,
For a lesson taught in pain, his love would never cease.
In the heart of the wilderness, where the air breathes free,
There lives a bond unbroken, a father and his daughter, forever to be.

McKenzie Bonar

The Female Experience

The mother and daughter in this cafe
move from small talk
to heartbreak
over overpriced coffee and tea.

The mother sits still, speaking calmly
and watches her daughter press
her nails into her paper coffee cup.

I watch as they set everything in them down
on the cafe table. They are both crying now.
The mother shifts her hand from her tea cup

to her daughter's arm. It trembles.

After a pause, at the same exact moment
the women look at each other and say,
"You didn't deserve that."

McKenzie Bonar

Birthday Wish

My Aunt Kay was supposed to die.
"For the past 20 years, that woman
has been dying," my dad says.

Aunt Kay and I celebrate
our birthdays together.
The 26th and 29th of January.
The worst of Pennsylvania winter.

Each year, Aunt Kay wishes on our candles
that it's her last.

When Aunt Kay was 68 her sister died.
Her sister wasn't supposed to die.
"I can't live without her," Aunt Kay said.

A year later Aunt Kay's husband died.
On her 70th birthday she begged,
"Please take me. I am ready."

Aunt Kay's liver functions at 13%
She has seizures and can't walk.
"What is keeping me down here
 so
damn
long?"

This year I beat her and blow out
all our candles,
wishing for one more year.

McKenzie Bonar

One more year for myself
and Aunt Kay together.
Because birthday candles
don't work when you reveal your wish.

McKenzie Bonar

A Doll's World

I smoke drunk cigarettes
because they "don't count when it's only one."

I rip my ballet tights from a decade ago into a shirt
as my girlfriend smudges her eyeliner onto my face.

I reread the same books over and over and over
so I don't have to be disappointed in an ending.

We take a walk to get fresh air and exercise
with vodka lemonades in our water bottles.

We research how to remove red wine stains from carpet
while the half empty bottles rest in our hands.

The girl I only met moments ago puts glitter on my eyelids.
She says to me, "We are so beautiful."

Autumn Buchheit

Wildflower

Cast through the wind by the days early breeze
Having no clue where the world might take thee
Fly through the sky with such beautiful ease
Oh how I wish that I could be that free
The personality of bravery
Standing up against all extremes they face
Held within them is what I do envy
Landing where they may is something I chase
They stand strong and grow tall, so beautiful
Their roots may be shallow, but they are fierce
Look out at the fields, they'll be plentiful
Still bright after hot, cold weeks, days and years
Wish that I could be a wildflower
Something that holds so much power

Kate Cramer

I am From Everything

I am the dust from a hundred years ago culminated in the abandoned historical homes
The tarnish of the slick train tracks at the edge of town, blocking the exit and entrance
I sit waiting at the train-crossing every morning as one, two, five, thirteen train cars crawl past
While I tap the wheel of my car, my own brakes are also resistant and squeaky with age.

I am from dirtied white sneakers and wearing something you don't mind getting messy in.
I am from straw hats and blistering golden summer sun on the hottest day of July,
Pink and blue plaid shorts stained with grass and dirt
Kneeling in front of my grandfather's garden.
I am from the small tomatoes that aren't quite ripe yet
That I still pick and squeeze between my fingers
Because curiosity was never a crime.

I'm from rule following
From scribbled drawings on the fridge and report cards displayed in homemade picture frames,
But I'm also from muggy late nights
Circling the same parking lot I've driven in a million times
The bright lights painting my silhouette with a warm yellow
Sometimes with friends in the backseat and other times
Alone.

Kate Cramer

I am from wooden porches painted rusty red every June
Wearing the same uniform of my dad's marked up Steelers shirt.
I am from the porch swing that squeaks like the brakes of my car with
    each rock
From the chipped lilac toe-nail polish my mom stretches to touch up
From the fireflies flickering on and off in the backyard.

I am from late night TV and old hard-covered children's books.
I am spilled soda and messy paint and glass cleaner and broken crayons
I am the useless chain of my childhood bike in the shed
I am the town I drive into every morning with the old brick buildings
    and one-way streets.
I am fresh cut grass on a Saturday in December
I am another story for a neighbor to tell their neighbor because everyone
    knows everything around here.

I am from the sincerest form of love
that I've only been able to find in my Grandmother's house on a Sunday
    afternoon for family dinner.
I am from the warmth of the furnace kicking on for the first time that
    year.
I am from everything.

Kate Cramer

A Pirate's Note Home

To me darlin' Ma and Pa,
I write with stolen ink.
How I love a lack of law,
and looted ale to drink.

I write to you with my feet in sand
in hopes to reach you soon.
If I'm caught writing home,
I'm sure to be marooned.

So with this stolen ink,
a kiss to the parchment, too,
I'll watch the bottle sink,
and pray it will wash up safely for you.

I watch the glistening bottle
with the parchment tucked away.
I watch it bob up and down
'til it washes up next to me.

I'm sorry Ma and Pa,
I won't be home for Christmas or even guarantee
that I'll be safe or abide by law
Because my home is here, at sea.

Caitlin Cruser

two friends and I got haircuts on thursday

we sat in the chairs
capes on our shoulders
looking older than we ever have

my stylist
robyn
sprays down my flyaways
with a bottle of conditioner and water

she smells like cigarettes and rain
I close my eyes and she parts my hair
"my last day is sunday,"
she says

she will go to the next town over
to cut hair for 11.75
plus tips

"what are we doing today?"
she asks

in 5 months I'll graduate
ceili will transfer
and cole will go back to south hills

but today
we are doing long layers

the scissors float around my head
and clipped hairs fall on my nose

Caitlin Cruser

behind me
cole has taken off his glasses
there's an indent on either side of his nose

ceili's stylist is holding her hair
to simulate curtain bangs
our eyes meet in the mirror
and she nods

when we are done
we pay
and leave big tips

we are both young
and old

both rich
and poor

we are alive
and we are friends
and we have new haircuts

Caitlin Cruser

when I hear the word 'yinz'
I think of Pittsburgh and its terrible beauty
and the man who towed my car for cheap
because it was in such shit shape

his dirty callused hands
moving papers off the passenger seat
and 8 walkie-talkies on the dash
picking up police radio frequencies

I think of the city
and its tough love

its wide open arms
that come with a lecture
and the man who told me
I was driving the wrong way on bouquet street

he said "you're going to get fucking arrested"
he said "I don't want you getting hurt"

Caitlin Cruser

annie

annie can't pay for college
but you wouldn't know it
she takes expensive clothes off the racks
checks for security tags
before stuffing them in her wide tote
stitches ripping

annie works for a sandwich shop
but won't call it a job
calls it something to do
besides drinking
and studying her anatomy notes

she gets a free sub and a bag of chips each shift

annie hasn't paid for a book in 3 months
she hasn't paid for facewash in 6

annie knows the workers don't get paid enough
to follow her out of the store
because annie is the worker

and she doesn't

and she won't

Cole Drusbasky

Poetry and Bourbon

do I actually enjoy poetry?
I ponder as I pour
more bourbon into my glass.

there is never a topic
that comes to mind
when I am writing poems.
so, I end up writing bizarre things.

when a topic finally arrives
I can't finish the thought
because I just finished
my last bit of bourbon.

Cole Drusbasky

The Dad Image

This morning, I was in a rush
so I quickly put on some dirty clothes
and went to work.

As I was sitting at my desk working, drinking coffee,
I saw my reflection in the window.
I realized that looked like someone's father.
Three-day-old jeans, white sneakers, and a stained white crewneck.

I felt like a dad
who, on a cool, damp Sunday morning, got up early
to make some quick phone calls
and would later repaint the upstairs hallway.

Drinking black coffee from his favorite mug,
listening to the strange silence from the rest of the house,
and enjoying the sounds of his brush against the wall.

He might step outside
for a slow drag of a cigarette,
feeling the cool breeze that comes
during the period between summer and autumn.

Daddy's Drugs

I was outside drinking beer with two eighth graders. Jewel and Butch were official teenagers, but I was only twelve. Butch crushed his can with his beefy hands and threw it on the grass.

"That beer tasted like piss," Butch said. Butch was the only kid on our block who was over six feet. Most of the kids hid whenever they saw Butch coming.

"You taste like piss!" I said.

"You just got burned!" Jewel yelled. Jewel was so skinny that the wind could blow him away.

"Shut up, Jewel. That doesn't count," Butch said.

"He's just mad because he knows I'm right," I said. I'd been getting better at comebacks ever since I started hanging out with Jewel and Butch. These guys were the masters of insults, and they'd hold comeback battles during recess. They called me background because I wasn't quick enough to come up with a cool remark, so I would always repeat what Butch said.

"Shut up, Background or I'll beat you up," Butch said.

"You're too fat to beat me up. I could knock you out with my eyes closed," I said.

Butch stood up and yanked my shirt.

"Uh, relax, I was just joking, man," I said.

Butch let me go and I sighed.

"There's nothing to do out here. This place is so boring," Jewel said after tossing his beer can on someone's lawn.

"We should go to my house. I got drugs," I said.

"You're lying, Background," Butch said.

"No, I'm not. I found some in my dad's room," I said.

Butch and Jewel smoked pot during recess. I wasn't sure where they got it from, but they made fun of me for weeks because I wouldn't smoke with them. The other day I discovered my dad's weed stash and his bong.

"You're too pussy to smoke drugs anyway. Why should we believe you?" Jewel asked.

"I've smoked before. I'm just tryna cut back," I said.

"Go bring your dad's drugs," Butch said.

I ran to my house and headed upstairs to get my dad's pot. He wouldn't get home till six, so my chances of getting caught were low. Dad was an exterminator, who spent most of the day killing bugs and destroying bee hives. He usually came home after sundown. I entered his room and searched his drawers for the weed. When I walked in, the black comforter was bunched up and the white pillows were scattered on the white carpet. The walls were covered in doodles I made when I was in preschool. I found the stash, which was wrapped in a brown bag. I grabbed his bong and sprinted out of the house.

I showed my dad's drugs to Jewel and Butch. They inspected it a couple of times and both of them were amazed.

"Background wasn't lying. His dad's got pot," Butch said.

"We gotta smoke this shit. Butch, do you have a lighter?" Jewel said.

Butch checked both of his pockets.

"Nah, I ain't got one. I know they sell that shit at 7-Eleven."

"Aye, Background, go get us a lighter," Butch said.

"Uh, I don't get my allowance till next week," I replied.

"You're a dumbass, Background. Just go steal it," Jewel said.

I didn't think twice, and I was already on my way to 7 eleven. I couldn't fuck this up. If I smoked pot with Jewel and Butch, they'd stop calling me Background. I'd be a legend to all the other seventh graders and I wouldn't have to eat lunch by myself.

The biggest issue was getting in and out of 7-Eleven without getting caught. I'd never stolen from a gas station. Jewel and Butch stole shit all the time. They even went into movie theaters without paying for a ticket. I wanted to be crafty like them, but sometimes I felt like a big klutz. I didn't belong in the background, and I had to prove that to them.

I found the lighter near the beer section. Butch and Jewel smuggled beer in their lunch boxes and that's how I started drinking it. Our school was for being the worst middle school in the district. There were daily fights and kids would slap teachers or randomly send an email that there was a bomb in the hallway. During recess, the teachers would pretend to supervise us, so it wasn't difficult for Jewel and Butch to sneak beer on the playground. I snatched the lighter and pretended like I was shopping for other things.

When the cashier left, I dashed out of the store. I came back to Jewel and Butch, who were staring at the weed.

"Damn, that was quick," Butch said.

"It's too hot to smoke out here. Let's do this inside," Jewel suggested.

"We can smoke it in my basement," I said.

Butch and Jewel followed me to my house. Each house had a freshly cut lawn with a picket fence. This was the kind of neighborhood where everyone went to the same church, and they hosted holiday parties together. Our basement had a dull gray brick wall, and I heard a squeaking noise every time I went down the steps. Jewel hopped on the lumpy brown couch, while Butch and I sat on the lawn chairs. Butch lit the weed on the brown table that was in the middle of the room. He took a hit and passed the bong to Jewel. Jewel took his own and handed it to me. I couldn't believe this was happening. I was officially about to become cool. I grabbed the bong but struggled to get a flame. I finally got a hit, and I started coughing.

Butch and Jewel shook their heads.

"Man, I knew you were lying," Butch said.

"He can't even handle it," Jewel said.

They started snickering, while my cool reputation was slipping away. We continued to smoke, and I got used to the feeling. Everything felt super slow, and I saw Jewel kick his head back.

Butch rubbed his stomach, and said, "I'm starving, man. You got anything to eat, Background?"

"My name is Monty," I said.

"Shut up, Background," Jewel said in a slow voice.

"Yeah, go get us some food or I'm gonna kick your ass," Butch said, and he laughed so hard that he fell out of his chair.

My stomach started growling, so I got up to hunt for food. I headed to the kitchen and opened the fridge. I kept opening and closing it, hoping a large pizza would appear. I heard the front door open, and my mom walked in.

"Monty, I'm home!" Mom said. Mom walked in with several grocery bags. Mom was wearing red scrubs and scuffed white Nike shoes. She worked odd hours at the hospital, which made it difficult to predict when she'd come home. I don't know how she still got groceries and did most of the chores while saving lives in the ER.

I immediately took the bags and searched for snacks.

"Can I get a greeting?" Mom said.

"Sorry, Mom, but my friends and I are hungry," I said.

"Oh, that's nice. Can I meet them?" Mom said.

"No, they don't like grownups," I said.

"Monty, you shouldn't be ashamed of your mother," Mom said. Mom saw that the basement door was open, and she started sniffing.

"Ugh, what is that smell?" she said.

"It's my laundry," I said.

"No, it smells like smoke," Mom said in a worried tone. She ran downstairs and I dropped the groceries.

She saw Jewel and Butch rolling on the carpet. She grabbed the bong.

"Monty, where did you get this thing?" Mom said.

"I got it from Dad," I said.

Mom glanced at Jewel and Butch who had their feet in the air. "Get out of my house!" Mom yelled.

"Can we get some food first?" Jewel asked. Mom pointed at the stairs, and they ran out of the basement.

I had little hope that I'd be allowed to hang out with Butch and Jewel for the rest of the school year.

"Monty, tell me the truth. Where did you get this?" Mom said.

"Mom, I swear it's Dad's. I found it in his drawer," I said.

"That's it. You're grounded for three months, and I don't wanna see you hanging out with those hooligans!" Mom said.

Later that night, I heard Mom and Dad arguing. It was the reason I couldn't sleep even when I tried covering my ears with two pillows.

"So, you're a dope head now?" Mom said.

"Honey, I'm sorry you had to find out this way. I've just been stressed at work and the weed helps me calm down," Dad said.

"There's a million fucking ways to reduce stress, Darius. Why did you have to turn to pot?" Mom said.

My parents continued to argue for the rest of the night. The fighting didn't stop there. Mom was considering filing for divorce since she felt like Dad broke her trust. I couldn't bear to hear my parents bicker every night.

I didn't mind getting grounded. I'd see Butch and Jewel again and hanging out with them was better than listening to my parents argue all day. Dad was right about one thing; Weed takes the pain away.

Orlando Gannon

On Dying

Dreams are dashed;
thoughts are left
wide open.

They dissolve
like sunlight
over volcanic sand
and are washed away.

The Soul is swept
down the shore of history.
Gleaming and bright,
and eager to embrace the sea.

Grateful,
at last,
to be home.

Orlando Gannon

Following the Wrong God Home

What does this little bug
have to teach me
about god?

It thrashes itself against
hurricane lantern glass,
desperate to slake
it's thirst for the light.

I'm sympathetic.

I have also
mistaken paraffin
for moonbeams
and gotten lost in the night.

I understand, little one.
I understand, believe me.

Your furious effort
and earnest intent
earn recycled failure.
Failure.
Failure.

Denied your destiny by cruel and invisible forces.
Shame creeps in
through the cracks
in your armor.

You get dizzy,
and forget what you're doing.

"May I make a humble suggestion?" I interrupt.

Orlando Gannon

"Sit down for a moment.
Catch your breath
and have a look around.

There's something
by the window...
it may be of interest."

Orlando Gannon

Reflections

I remember my reflection
In the triplicated mirrors
of a department store
fitting room.

All I felt, at first
was confusion.
surely, it couldn't
be me...could it?

Some fat kid
had wandered in.
Maybe from a long day
at Disneyland.

All puffy and shiny
and red-faced.
Swollen by high-octane
corn syrup
and hydrogenated vegetable oils—
and a life of
hyponormal reward:
maximal gratification; minimal dedication.

Jesus, do I really
look like that?
I probed the depths
of my reflections as they
assaulted my senses
from new and creative vectors—repeating their message in
infinitely regressing
fractals of shame.

Where were the heroic
and manly features of
my film and television
mentors?
I thrust out my chin,
and sucked in my belly.
And for naught.
I looked down.

If I could whisper through time, into that boy's ear,
I might say:
"You tubby little Angel,
don't despair.
Life is dynamic;
nothing lasts forever.

Someday soon, I promise,
you'll begin to see
the warrior dwelling
even now,
waiting to be embodied.

Now be good.
Don't tell lies.
Work hard.
Look after your sister.
I love you."

Orlando Gannon

Hunting Tigers

Hunting Tigers
is dangerous Business.
Stalking stripes
stalking back
with keener eyes
and devouring quickness.

Lighting fires
of greed is unstable.
Plain men
see plainly
this world
you have made us
is flimsy,
a fable.

That's enough, old friend
they're already dead!
You've had your
fun; we've had enough—
let's play a different
game instead.

Your verse means nothing
 to a drowning man.
What use are swords and pens?
Stop writing,
And lend the poor fellow
your hand!

You forget,
we've survived a thousand
battles—
wars fought without

Orlando Gannon

malice or reason.
Please,
take a moment
to look around--
before speaking one's
mind is made treason.

Cole Drusbasky

"Somewhere in Greensburg"

Cole Drusbasky

"Somewhere Else in Greensburg"

Sophia Gatti

mt. washington outlook / pittsburgh, pa

the breeze that blows
through my body,
when up at the outlook,
is a delightful, divine
almost dust-like feeling.

when staring past the dark,
the city looks luminating.
like there is hope.
there it is!
there is the chance of change
you have been praying for.

i swear at night,
there is magic floating
all through the air,
within the place you stand
to view this cultured city.

mt. washington to me
is a place to go to feel again.
a place to go to reconnect with my light-side.
a place that friends and i
 scattered mary-jane smoke
and discussed just why we fucking loved
every part of pittsburgh, pa.

cigarette butts

to me your return is evil.
to me your return is low.
the day you left,
you should have seen your face.
you should have seen
the shallowness embedded in your eyes.
every vile memorable sting
you left behind,
right next to every cigarette butt
 you left on the grass.

and now you come back
with the shallowness buried and hidden.
just like i did with
every vile sting.

just so you know,
that summer i watched
the sunbeams break those
leftover cigarette ends into pieces.
that fall i watched
the rain wash them away.
so please,
be like the ends you left
and vanish.

Monroe Harris

led down the primrose path

the phone line cut dead
i had no real chance to plead my case
just the bitter taste of betrayal
hanging onto the words i was about to say
the ringing dial tone
in agreement with my words left unspoken

you may try to erase me
with the borrowed sweatshirts
and fleeting affections
of the next prize you lay your eyes on
but what happens when they expire
in a few months too?
because darling, soon you'll realize
lightning like that won't strike again for you

when that happens, your thousand-yard stare
won't work on me
your map to the blue skies
where i could once be found
is now buried deep alongside your memory
i left our love on the cutting room floor
but i see you haven't even left the screening

you'll keep my polaroid and notes
deep in your bottom drawer
but darling, how much longer can you continue to live on
hiding your head from what's in your heart?
you had my heart
but i fear now i've taken yours

i know i am new to love
but my wide-eyed naivety can't be to blame

Monroe Harris

when you used "you're my everything" as a prelude
just three days before ending things
i wish i trusted myself to be hesitant
to call it forever
but you wrote it on paper like it was law
but who could ever guess
that three days is long enough
to decide three months
but i guess only a coward slams an open door shut

Julia Hills

Learning to Drive with my Mostly Deaf Grandad in a Truck from the '90s in the Parking Lot of the AMC in the Waterfront.
I long for the feeling of the engine rumble, the smell of my grandparent's house melted into the seats, and the sound of my Grandad humming a tune he learned in the army.

I'll never forgive him for selling his truck.

Or dying.

Julia Hills

Aging on the Internet

I'm young enough to have never used a floppy disk, but old enough to know what one is, and yet somehow, I still can't figure out why I never have storage on my phone.

Siblings

"Come along Jake," 17-year-old Emma yells at her younger brother as she gets him out of the backseat.

"I want to go to F.Y.E.," Jake crosses his arms and places his feet firmly on the ground in a stomp. "Mom said you're buying a DVD for me. Promise is a promise."

"Yeah, I know, but we have to go to Macy's first, then we can eat, and go there after," Emma impatiently locks her 2006 Subaru Forester. "We have to see my friend for lunch in 20 minutes."

"I want my DVD," Jake now runs behind her as they speed walk to the entrance of Macy's. "Mom said..."

"I KNOW what mom said, but just this one time can you not complain? We will be going there later."

"*Fine*," Jake says as he immediately takes off his coat once they enter the store.

"No, Jake. Leave your coat on; You can leave it unzipped. If you lose it, dad will yell at mom who will then yell at me," Emma says as she forces his right arm back into the coat.

"I hate coats," Jake yells loudly as he pulls the hood up.

"I hate them too but we have to wear them. Quit yelling, put it on *now*," Emma whisper yells at him. He puts his arm in and gives her an evil glare from under the hood.

"You better keep that dang coat on or else," Emma gives him a stern pat. "Mom says it's expensive." She has to make sure not to cuss or else their dad would have a chat with her about it later if Jake started repeating after her.

"*Fine*, let's go already," Jake pouts.

Jake is 14 and has high-support Autism, which is always a sore subject for Emma. Their mom has put a lot of emphasis on Emma needing to care for Jake ever since she got a boyfriend who has his own kids she seems to like more. When their mom has her custody day, instead of giving them her time, she forces Emma to parent and take Jake with her. Jake always acts less than half his real age due to Autism's effects. She always finds his public outbursts and rudimentary ways very upsetting and embarrassing when she is just trying to get a task done or help him do his tasks. Jake has no idea how much of an impact he has on Emma, and all she wants is for him to behave, but that feels like a tall order on this snowy Friday at East Hills Mall.

The siblings leave Macy's, her homecoming dress in tow, and head all the way down the large hall towards the food court to meet her friend Maddy. Fortunately for Emma, F.Y.E. is not down this wing or else she would have to drag him past it, which is nearly impossible now that he is almost as tall as she is.

"Okay, here's the plan Jake, we are going to order our food and then meet Maddy in 10 minutes - it won't be hard," Emma is now grasping his hand trying to lead him through the mass of people walking in the opposite direction.

"Maddy? I like Maddy, but I don't want food, I want my DVD," Jake shouts as he stops walking and stands rooted like a tree. Emma hanging on to him nearly falls forward from the sudden stoppage. People are now staring as they walk past.

"*Jake, Stop*. I've had enough of this. I told you the plan and that we will be going after we *eat*. Mom was the one who made you come with me, so you have to follow the plan. You like plans anyways so why are you fussing?"

"I'm not fussing," Jake now clasps his hands to his ears, which he does when he is trying to ignore someone.

"Do not embarrass yourself in this dang hallway, besides you like Maddy and Auntie Anne's so..?" Emma says as she places her hands on her hips standing in front of him.

"I'll only do it if you get me ice cream too," Jake pouts. "Dad always gets it for me."

"Ugh, whatever then, we can't be late," Emma says as she grabs his hand and they begin to walk again. Emma being relieved he didn't try and lay down on the dirty floor this time and that his coat is actually still on him even though the hood is up.

They arrive at the food court and go up to the Auntie Anne's counter. It smells of fresh pretzels and lemonade and the ovens ringing.

"Go on and order, you're old enough, and you practice it in school. I'll hand you the money," Emma says as she hands him a $10 bill their mom gave them to share for Christmas.

"Here, split this $10 when you go to the mall," their mom told her as Emma got her coat on to leave with Jake that morning. "Oh, and merry late Christmas. Maybe next year spend it here instead."

"But why would I spend Christmas here when you fail to even get us at least one nice gift to actually open while his kids get the entire toy aisle under the tree?" Emma retorts.

"Get on out, I need to take the kids to daycare," their mom spits as she goes to light her cigarette. "Oh, and don't forget, you two are leaving the mall and going *straight* back to your dad's; I won't be here."

Fine, Emma thought

"Thanks for the reminder," Emma had said as she ushered Jake out the door and into the back seat. Him humming the whole way there.

"One regular pretzel, no cheese, and a sprite," Jake says as the top of the hood stares the employee in the face.

"Remember to say please," Emma prompts as she stands off behind him.

"Please," he whispers.

"Sure, is that all," asks the employee.

"Is it," Jake turns around to Emma.

"Yes," Emma nods.

"YES," Jake yells.

"It'll be ready in a minute," the employee says as he hands Emma the change. "Here's your cup to fill your own drink."

Jake looks fearfully at the cup.

"They didn't give me any drink Emma," Jake says sadly.

"You have to pick your own here, see these taps?"

"But they don't have sprite," Jake's face starts to get red and you can see he's about to become upset. Emma panics.

"They don't have sprite but they have 7 UP. it's similar to Sprite, or maybe you can try another soda instead!"

"I don't WANT another soda, Emma," He is gripping the paper cup hard now and an indent has formed where the middle of the pretzel on the cup is. "I want *my* Sprite. Mom said you'd buy me Sprite."

"Well maybe we can get Sprite where I order then," Emma says. He calms down. *Another embarrassing outburst avoided* she thinks.

They get his food and stop by Subway to get hers. Fortunately, they have Sprite and the employee generously allows them to get a cup of Sprite for a few cents extra.

They find Maddy already sitting at a table in the center of the neon-lit court. Maddy has been Emma's biggest support and the only person her age to be accepting towards hanging out with Jake. After many instances of embarrassment in front of her former friends who told

Emma that she wouldn't be invited anymore, Emma doesn't love the idea of sitting with Jake in public due to his unpredictable behavior. In the past, he has thrown food around when upset or turned around and nearly knocked over something or someone.

"Hi Emma, Hi Jake," Maddy smiles and shifts over to leave room to the side of her.

Emma and Jake sit. He always insists on the booth side, and Emma decides to sit on the adjacent side in between him and Maddy, so that way she can keep him in arms reach if need be.

Jake begins to eat, and he always eats very aggressively and loudly. Nothing Jake ever does is silent and it worries Emma that people around them will stare.

"Eat quieter Jake," Emma tugs at him. "You don't need to talk like SpongeBob while you eat."

Jake just stares and rocks back and forth and demolishes a quarter of the pretzel while quoting the "He was #1" line from an episode. Emma wonders if Maddy feels embarrassed or uncomfortable, but fortunately, Emma sees her smile.

"Sorry, we were a little late. He almost had a meltdown when they had no Sprite," Emma tells Maddy and shakes her head. "Then he wouldn't walk in the hallway, and so I have to get him ice cream now."

"Sorry Emma, it must be hard," Maddy sighs. "I know you probably feel embarrassed in front of everyone when he gets mad, but it's not your fault and at least he's calm now."

"I guess for now," Emma stares at Jake as he chugs the Sprite. "I just wish my mom would understand like my dad does that I don't want to be a parent. I can't be."

***

They go to leave the food court and say goodbye to Maddy. They stop and get ice cream and head on down to F.Y.E. Emma is quite proud of Jake, because he ordered his own ice cream and her order too and kept an inside voice - a rarity for him.

"Let's go to F.Y.E. now Jake and get your movie," Emma says as she takes his hood off that he kept putting on. It's either coat off or the hood is on apparently.

"It's not a movie, it's a TV show," he says pointedly as he holds his fists up in such a way that makes him look like a T-Rex. He begins to set off running and Emma has to run, dress bag in hand, and yell for him to slow down. He nearly runs into an elderly woman mall walker who gives him a mean glare.

"Sorry!" Emma yells back at her. Her face turned hot with embarrassment.

"Not sorry!" Jake yells as he continues to run. He shimmies his coat off and it falls in front of Emma. She picks it up as he runs inside the store.

"You need to take care of that kid," the elderly lady screams back at Emma.

Ugh, Emma thinks. *Tell it to our "mom".*

He goes in immediately to the rack where his DVD should be.

Emma catches up and pauses for a breath and asks rhetorically "What are you looking for?"

"I'm looking for *The Office*: *Season 4*," Jake says as he picks through every DVD as each one slaps against the one in front of it.

"Does dad know you watch that show? He probably wouldn't want you to see some of that stuff; It's not always age appropriate for you."

"Mom said as long as dad hates it, I can watch it," Jake laughs, and is now frantically searching for it. He's flipping through them like a Rolodex. Apparently he is in the last row of where it should be.

"THEY DON'T HAVE IT"

"Well, maybe we can ask the employee and if not, then maybe you can pick another one out or we can order it and they can have it shipped in for you," Emma says nervously.

"NO."

"Fine, but I am NOT letting you yell and throw a fit here. Don't make me have to call mom and disrupt her. You know how she feels about me calling her for help."

Jake has some violent tendencies, but their mother never sees it as a bother. Not even when the aide at school sent home a letter of recommendation for extra behavioral services. Emma remembered that their dad had asked her to come to the IEP meeting about it, but she wouldn't.

"You should be there for Jake and Emma more like you are for his kids," their dad said as he called their mom from the car on the ride to the meeting that afternoon.

"Jake's just a child, and Emma? She's old enough to handle things on her own and take care of him," their mom countered, as Emma had sat passenger next to her dad and thought of her mom holding hands with her step kids like how she used to hold theirs.

"You can't just make Emma a caregiver for him while you spend all your supposed allotted time with them with his children instead," their dad scolded as their mom hung up.

Their mom always hangs up on them.

Jake is yelling and starting to throw a few DVDs. Emma tries to control his hands, but is failing.

An employee starts to walk over to try to help and make peace seemingly understanding Jake's autism, but while Emma is distracted by the employee, he punches her in the side of the nose.

Emma tries to get her bearings back while the employee asks if she is okay and another tries to hold Jake back as he screams. A third calls for their security guard to come help de-escalate. Emma can't feel her face, but she walks over to Jake, and with a flash of strength, pulls him by the flailing arms out of the store. Security meets them and kindly helps them back to their car. Emma thinks to herself as she gets him buckled in the backseat, *I'm never coming back here with you again.*

Jeanette Hutzell

The Dog Didn't Actually Die That Year, By the Way...
The dog fell in the ice-cold pond and dad thinks she has bronchitis,
which is fine because she's ancient
and she should probably be put out of her misery
like dad's old truck that stopped working last week.

He fished her out on christmas eve
so the next day I opened gifts while listening to her hack
echoing from downstairs, wrapped up in an old quilt
that should probably be put down too.

But this family never gives up on things
even when we should, but especially when we shouldn't
and last christmas I really wanted to die
but now its 9 p.m. and I'm spending the night huddled
against an old, smelly farm dog I've known since I was three
thankful my parents don't give up on tarnished things.

Jeanette Hutzell

An Old Hag

She pops her feet up on an old bucket
and shucks a knife over an oak branch
scanning the land in front of her.

It's an old cabin in the crook of the woods,
bleeding moss from its old bones
and holding her fifty years of belongings.

Her face is haggard and worn from years
and the kids write stories about its skin,
sneaking into her yard to get inspiration.

And because of their peculiar game
she peers out from the shaded porch
like an old hawk with ratted wings

until she spots one in the foliage,
darting away with a flash of pale white
like a tiny field mouse.

She rises up with her walking stick
throwing it in the air to shriek,
"Stay out of my lawn."

One day,
I think warmly,
I will be her.

Jeanette Hutzell

Small Town U.S.A

Barely desirable on
shitty two dollar holiday cards.

It took me forty five minutes
to get to Walmart
and ten more to get my grandad
to the hospital
when he had a heart attack.
But in a local drug store
with our cult paraphernalia
"Sweetest Place on Earth"
poor is a way of life
everyone buys with coupons.

Cole Drusbasky

"Brayden"

Benjamin Keslar

Death And Taxes

It was in the middle of a bright, clear day when they gathered for the seance. They'd had to put up blackout curtains to ensure they could go through with it; while seances can be held in broad daylight it's far, far easier in flickering darkness. Candles are traditional, but they'd blown most of their budget on the curtains and the cage, so they had to use an ancient CRT one of them had found in their basement. It's condition hardly mattered; no one was broadcasting, and they'd intended to light this room with static anyway. The glow was quite nice, an eerie, cold light, but the infrasonic hum of the machine's electron gun was more headache-inducing than spinechilling. The white noise, at least, added enough chaos for stochastic resonance to kick in.

"Let us begin."

The medium sat opposite the TV, staring into it. This allowed her, as well as the technicians sitting beside her, a good view of any electromagnetic distortions on the screen. Ghosts, of course, emit an electromagnetic field; that's just elementary parapsychology. They all held hands, gathering in a heptagon around a circular table, with the TV on another, smaller table off to the side.

"We gather here today to contact the spirit of Archibald Fitzgerald."

The medium continued. Everyone closed their eyes at this point and focused as best they could on what the medium was saying. This was no mean feat, considering the TV's buzzing.

"Archibald Fitzgerald, please join us here today."

There was a few more seconds of static before they started to notice the voices in the noise.

"Archibald Fitzgerald, are you here with us?"

They all heard the whispering now, and eyes began to open.

The TV began to flash on and off in morse code.

- • - -   •   • • •

One of the bureaucrats who'd joined as table-filler knew morse, and translated it in their head:

Y E S

"Archibald Fitzgerald, you owe the IRS fifteen million two hundred fifty seven thousand eight hundred twenty three dollars in back taxes accumulated over the past ten years. Please tell us where you kept your money."

Once more the TV flashed, on and off.

•• -•   -•-- ---   ••- •-•   •- ••• •••

Whispered and transcribed:

I N

Y O U R

A S S

"Archibald, we can do this the easy way or the hard way."

••-• ••- -•- ••-

F U K

U

The interrogator began to ready himself, the clink of chainmail adding to the noise.

"Archibald James Fitzgerald, reveal yourself, or be held in contempt."

- • - - -

N O

"Archibald James Fitzgerald, by the power of the United States of America, it's constitution and all of its federal laws and statutes, reveal yourself and be held in contempt."

That worked, finally. The TV stopped flashing, but changed, distorted into faces in the static.

A humanoid distortion began to form in the center of the table, a penumbral shadow man.

As it solidified, the TV went out, and they were enshrouded in seemingly total darkness.

I say seemingly because they'd forgotten to block out the cracks beneath the doors. This let in a miniscule level of light, not enough to be noticed when the TV was on but enough to see by once their eyes had adapted. It was clear, in the monochrome near-infra-red of natural night vision, that Archibald Fitzgerald had manifested fully in the middle of the table.

It was at that moment that the left technician stomped his foot down on the button, and the cage dropped.

Fitzgerald was now trapped in a Faraday Cage. Ghosts, after all, emit electromagnetic fields; that's just basic parapsychology.

The TV turned back on, and the seance was adjourned. But the job still wasn't done. In less than an hour the technicians had covered the walls in several layers of aluminum foil, and bolted in shielded door, turning the room into a larger cage. The walls were now silvery, lit by LED spotlights. In The center, still on top of the circular table, was the ghost, an apparition with the appearance of a bloated, eyeless corpse, held in the inner cage.

The plan was to sweat it out; ghosts can't die, but they diminish over time into oblivion, and they do so painfully fast when they sustain a form for extended periods. Unless, of course, they possess some outside source of energy.

...

It took several days for the ghost to give them any usable information. In that time the police had finished investigating, cleaned up, and clearly ruled the man's death as a suicide. No note was found.

The information was a list of five addresses, all the sites owned by Fitzgerald.

The first was a factory; it had been closed for many years by this time, left to the elements. After tearing the place apart they found a corpse, half mummified, in a broom closet. DNA analysis indicated that it was a relative of Fitzgerald, likely a child of his to an unknown mother. Dead by a gunshot wound to the back of the head; the bullet matched a revolver Fitzgerald had owned. Their eyes had been removed with a spoon.

The other addresses went similar; another place, another corpse. Most were relatives of Fitzgerald; some were children. In one place they'd found a room full of corpses, all children, unrelated. None of them had eyes.

The night afterward the medium stole the interrogator's gloves.

Ghosts cannot die, as they are already dead; that's just basic parapsychology. Ghosts cannot be destroyed from physical trauma; they cannot go into shock, pass out, or go numb. As such, it felt every ounce of pain even when she'd torn its form into a thousand pieces, and it was just as aware when she'd spread its form like butter against the inner cage.

Everyone else watched, without interference.

By the end it was flattened and stretched and misshapen. Yet still it was silent. For the first time since they'd started monitoring its facial expressions, it began to smile.

...

Ghosts usually can't maintain a full-bodied apparition for more than a week; even those held in Faraday cages or penning traps still decay into nonexistence within a few days.

Benjamin Keslar

By the third week they'd begun to figure that something was up.

They were running up to their deadline now and had begun to repo the house and its contents, to try to make this effort something more than a total loss. To ensure that they didn't auction off anything useful, they'd had the medium and the interrogator examine everything before it could be shipped away. That was where they found it, four mason jars full of eyes, preserved in formaldehyde. This would have to be it; everyone knew, even before the medium had confirmed it and the DNA had been traced and records had been matched, that these were the eyes of his victims.

Finally, with something of value to threaten, they returned to the outer cage. The jars had to be carried in in evidence bags; they would be turned over to the police after this had been done. The spirit stopped smiling as soon as the jars were brought in. They had his banking information before they could even begin to threaten.

Jed Kudrick

Level Green As Baseball

The baseball diamond erected at school
Where home plate could be home to all
Friends, families, classmates gathered for the big game
My teammates had each other as schoolfellows
I, homeschooled, had no one
but sometimes my friend, Paul, when we all left that field
So I played for my family's entertainment
more than for my own enjoyment
A time long gone, but the memories still here

No longer is the ding of bat hitting ball heard
The sound of a parent cheering their kid on

Across the street from my childhood home
So close but still so far
Connections long since severed
But emotions still buried inside

I can never return as I once was
But the games continue on still
The future generations now at bat
While the home plate is home to me no more
I wonder what my life would be like had I continued to play ball
A life with ambitions? Friendships? Pride?
I guess I'll never know as that route I did not follow
My teardrops stain this hallowed sand as I forever leave the dugout behind

The Fall: Monroeville: 18

Because ignorance ran through my veins
Because I was tired and couldn't think clearly
Because I was happy and carefree
Because I was stupid and made a mistake
Because I was sick of my job
Because forty hours, five days a week
Because I was training new people when I didn't even want to be there myself
Because the people were the only ones keeping me there
Because Kenz and her strategies to get us maximum tips
Because Jesse and his schemes try to cheat the system
Because I was promised a promotion to area leader
Because Lauren asked me to grab her something
Because I couldn't tell her no
Because I was then in the wrong place at the wrong time
Because I watched Tori and Taylee climb out the window and didn't stop them
Because the manager told me if I wanted to succeed to not become friends with them
Because I chose friends over power
Because I wouldn't subject myself to their authoritative whims
Because the owner chose his own profit over our personal feelings
Because money is not god to me
Because I had just moved out
Because I thought I was free
Because in the end my friends were all that mattered
Because late night hangouts in the work parking lot
Because all of our cars took up all of the spaces
Because we stayed there for hours in the cold just having fun
Because my best friend's naturally charismatic ways
Because his three most recent ex-girlfriends were all there at the same place, same time
Because the drama that that caused

Jed Kudrick

Because it'd been a long day and we were all out of it
Because we'd all been overworked
Because of a store owned by adults run by children
Because he was my best friend
Because his truck bed was empty
Because he was not paying attention
Because I thought it would be funny
Because he hit the gas and realization set in
Because I launched myself off the edge
Because I chose fun over fortune
Because I chose the supposedly wrong friends
Because I was too arrogant to accept my mistake
Because the fall was physical
Because the fall was metaphorical
Because in the end it would cost me
Because in the end it would break me
Because snap, crackle, pop
Because a pain tolerance, too high
Because a jump, too high
Because ignorance lead to a downfall
Because that could be taken quite literally
Because the distance to the pavement
Because the scratches on my hands
Because my fall was broken
Because that was not the only thing that was broken
Because I shattered a bone in my elbow
Because the doctors said it would never heal
Because I still suffer the effects of that to this day
Because in the end that was all that really mattered
Because I would never recover from that loss
Because all those events led to today
Because maybe I'm happier than I ever was
Because maybe I had to fall in order to rise anew

Jed Kudrick

The Glass

He was drinking
He was always drinking

She said that was the problem
That's probably what she was screaming about right now

She was always screaming
He couldn't hear her anyway
The buzzing in his brain was too loud
They always fought
He was numb to their fights

The glass in his hand became lighter as he drank the contents away
He sat in his armchair, king of the world, king of crap

He was so sick of her yelling
He just wanted her to shut up

There was nothing else in arm's reach
What good was the glass anyway?
It was empty
His eyebrows furrowed
Enough was enough
So he threw it
He threw it at her head

No sooner had the glass left his fingertips
than he regretted it immediately

But it was too late

The glass arced through the air
like a fastball to a catcher

Jed Kudrick

It caught a sunbeam as it flew
glinting its surface while it sailed

The glass connected with her skull
and shattered upon impact

Pieces of glass and flesh and blood
separated from their previous placements

As the glass broke so did his whole world

A memory he had wanted to forget
now being replayed before his eyes
the individual shards of glass
all reflecting his past in front of him

He was now not unlike his father
who drank and yelled and screamed
and beat them 'til they were black and blue
Why couldn't his mother just leave him?
Why couldn't she take them away?
Why was she so devoted
to a man so devoted to the glass?

The previously clear glass pieces
now stained and tainted red
distorting his vision through them

Seeing himself young and weak and helpless
Why hadn't he fought back?
Why hadn't he protected her?
But what could a child
do against a grown man?

Jed Kudrick

But he was no longer a child
He was the grown man now
Generations of armchairs and abuse
continued on through him

His life and soul filled up the glass
until he was drained empty, too

He was done, finished, the end

Alexis Osborne

Spotlight

What if my writing isn't good enough?
What if I make a mistake?
Yes, that idea is good.
No, that idea is too broad.
Remember your deadlines.
Stick to your word count.
Learn to be confident, learn to be professional.
Being put on display across a big stage, the internet.
What if they don't like me?
Get good quotes, ask the right questions.
Know your audience, without personally knowing them,
and make them hear you without even speaking.
Pretend you're undercover, but still identify who you are.
Story is coming together, time to publish soon.
That's a wrap! Or is it?

Alexander Ray

Death of Morale

True, I do practice the act of introversion quite a bit,
but why should I be blamed? To what am I to admit?

When I am not the transgressor in question?
I am not typically one to act in aggression

towards others in outward ways, I should say,
for, only in privacy, do I sometimes get irate,
never to those who desire to brighten my day
but rather to those who nourish from the hate,

For such creatures, as it pains me to claim,
seem only to grow, to fester in number by the hour,
corrupting the pure, convincing them they are the same,
that, despite the effort, all people are equally as sour.

You may call me cynical, but even still,
do be confident that I do not speak in vain
since it is not by my own design or will
that some tend to thrive from others' pain,

Nor that, sometimes, the weakest among the populace,
often those who are primarily afflicted,
are given no respite, no chance at joyfulness
and consequently cause more pain, their sorrows reflected.

An unfortunate truth, just as this may be,
it is not its existence which vexes me so
but rather how it perseveres, our acting carefree,
acting in ignorance, feeding the spiteful weeds we sow.

Alexander Ray

And so he was right, Voltaire was, when once he said
that those who believe blindly inevitably regress,
and commit atrocities, not caring who ends up dead,
pinning the blame on others, if only to digress.

Is this what it's come to? Rashness without rationale?
No, I fear it is far worse, for it is the Death of Morale.

Alexander Ray

Reflection

People always tell me that I look alright,
that my visage is a very pleasant sight.
But why, then, when I look at my reflection,
do I only see a monstrous complexion?

I try telling myself that this isn't true,
for I know I have it better than most do,
and when I look around to see their faces,
I know I must stand out in the right places.

Alexander Ray

Autumn

Trees starting to shed
Bright hues of red and orange
Pile on verdant grass
As the ebony crow glides
Through brilliantly crisp air.

Geneva Webber-Smith

ER waiting room

I have left my phone in the room where my mother will die
so I wait
for security to let me back up
one more time
before my grandma drives us home.
Tonight is summer like a closed fist:
hot, slick, waiting.
A woman with gauze-wrapped wrists
paces
she needs a ride
she has to go home
she has nowhere to go
she has no one to take her.
I cannot call her an uber to nowhere
without a phone. But I can hold her hand. Rub my thumb across her palm.

Please, whatever happens, wherever you are, remember:
I love you.
When you have no one else but waiting
I love you.

Geneva Webber-Smith

What are the twenty-something flavors in a Dr. Pepper?
When Ashlyn was born, did they make her to sit beside me on the couch
that we carried off the curbside—
did they make her to share a Dr. Pepper with me out of
a pink checkerboard mug?
Why are delicious things kept secret?

Can I be selfish and say

please,
can this all be for me?

Can I please fit all of my rotten, syrupy self
into a five-gallon bucket in the kitchen
to be rinsed with soap and vinegar til
all I can hold are these sweet
fermenting
memories?

Thank You Dr. Manning
Dr. Manning brought a shitty pot of dark roast and
pink paper cups to
American Constitutional Law
10:00 – 10:50 A.M. M/W/F and I
didn't read my cases today.

Sorry, Dr. Manning.

Lauren Hohol

"Fog Along the Footbridge"

Lauren Hohol

"Forge Ahead"

Paper Accordions and Pigs in Spaceships

The cleaning product in the cafeteria smelled nothing like any lemon I've come across, but exactly like every school cleaning solution. Our dance class was in St. Philip's school, an hour and a half away from our house. My mom and I waited in the cafeteria while my sister danced with the older girls on Wednesday night. Then, on Thursday nights, it was my turn to suffer through the torture of Miss Cathy, insisting through tears that I had practiced. Both of us always coming out with tougher hearts and stiff shoulders from holding hangers behind our backs. But on Wednesdays it was Liz's turn to be toughened up, and I got a whole hour to kill with mom.

We sat on the hard, cold, metal stools in the closed cafeteria. Sometimes my mom would let me sit on her lap for a while if I really complained about the chilly metal. After a while, we had no choice but to stand up and walk around. We chatted about kindergarten, and Zoboomafoo, and when those topics ran out, we still had 50 minutes left. We had to take matters into our own hands. We became creators in that big, vacant room. We became authors, writing stories of pigs and spaceships, (always some animal and spaceships) on tiny crinkled up scraps of paper torn from the documents in my mom's work bag. I became a musician, playing grand concerts for my mom with the tiny paper accordion she would fold for me. And after the concert's third or fourth encore, my mom introduced a new game where I would hop away from her, tile by tile, down the length of the cafeteria. And when I hoped back, there was more paper to write on. Sometimes I would write stories and my mom would illustrate, other times she would draw first, and I would have to make up a story from the pictures. I was free from the rules of spelling, and grammar, and physics, and reality. My sheep could talk, and ate ice cream, and never used commas. Sometimes my mom would write stories with me. She'd make a UFO steal the ice cream, or drop down a birthday cake with gravity beam from space. Those were the stories I liked best. And sometimes I'd sit on her lap and watch her soft freckled hands draw tiny detailed flowers and mice and aliens to bring our stories to life.

The whole room was ours, until about 10 minutes to seven, when all the other moms came back. It never occurred to me why the other moms never stayed. Now, I know they drove home, most lived about five or 10 minutes away. But while they went home to clean, and cook, and work, and relax, my mom and I sat under the fluorescent lights, not caring about the long drive back to our house.

I wonder what Liz did with mom when we drove up for my lessons the next day. Did they sit in that cafeteria making worlds of spiders with tap shoes and performing paper accordion duets?

Late Night Creations In the Bottom Bunk

The omipioos eat teeth. They rob the innocent tooth fairy and trap her in a cage. After, they wash it down with pickle juice, straight from the jar. The omipoos lips turn white with anger as your sister pinches her fingers together.

The omipoos visit their grandmas and swear until the grandmas' are paralyzed with shock! The only cure is to release their jaw, lightly pinching the corner of your sister's hand in between the thumb and the pointer finger. Otherwise, the omipoo grandmas will be frozen like that forever, and your sister's hand will start cramping from holding that position.

The omipoos are mostly nocturnal. They get into their mischief when Liz sneaks down from the top bunk. Their cousins, the obipoos, come out in the car, but they're not as fun. They have to be quiet while mom is driving, so usually they don't stay out very long.

I believe the omipoos had their own theme song at some point. But for the life of me, I can't remember what it was. It hasn't been sung for many years.

The omipoos lost their habitat. The bunkbeds were taken down long before Liz moved miles away.

I wonder what the omipoos are doing now. I hope they're eating teeth and drinking pickle juice in whatever form someone else's imagination creates.

Florence Zhang

Dear T,

I wonder why I become so different around you,
and I know,
most partners would hate to hear those words.
Yet, I say them to you
in the most endearing way.

Why is it
that certain trios of words,
I find so difficult to say to others
spill so naturally from
my lips
when it comes to you.

I like you.
I want you.
I love you.

Why is it
that these things I never say,
you hear so often
to the point where
my mind
worries if you'll ever become sick of them.

I wonder why I become so different around you,
and I remember,
one of our first dates over at your place.
Where you said those trios of words to me
in the most endearing way.

Florence Zhang

My Father Now Resting

In spite of himself,
my father loved me. In spite
of the hands that gave me hush money
of the mouth that fed me lies, in spite
of the face that slowly began to sink and darken
as a star that has run out of fuel,
he could not control the love
that came out of him.

Whether it was his
love for writing, or
his love for people, he
never failed to keep a smile.

The body is hollow, a cavern
through which his breath echoes.
His hands quietly lie over his stomach
still as stone;
he lays
like that of the one he rests underneath.

Florence Zhang

The Good Old Dogs

I drop the fluffy beds down on the floor,
and they land with a low plop

I throw some small treats
for the good old dogs;

    they love the sound
of the *crunch crunch crunch*, and they will
never really savor the taste, since
they're gone in mere seconds;

    then they flop down,
with a light deflating sound of the air between the white cotton,
coming out of the cracks of the woven fabric,
the sound intertwining with the sound of their small sighs (which my
mother quietly laughs at)

        and their eyes flutter closed.

Sharp yet soft,
their faces
like little wolf pups.

Celli Schiller

"Overgrowth"

Celli Schiller

"Tandem Living"

Made in the USA
Middletown, DE
22 March 2024